Unicuique qui se umquam contemni aut despici sensit.

For everyone who's ever felt misjudged or misunderstood.

Published by Frog, Ltd.

Frog, Ltd. books are distributed by North Atlantic Books, P.O. Box 12327, Berkeley, California 94712

ISBN 1-58394-110-X

Book design by Audrey Colman and Paula Morrison
Translated by Robert Dobbin

Printed in Singapore

1 2 3 4 5 6 7 8 9 / 08 07 06 05 04

William Kotzwinkle et Glenn Murray

Walter Canis Inflatus

picturis ab Audrey Colman collatis

in sermonem Latinum ab Roberto Dobbin conversus

Frog, Ltd.
Berkeley, California

Betty et Billy Walterum domum adduxerunt electum ex ceteris canibus foras abiectis.

"Nemini placuit," Billy dixit.

"Nos autem" inquit Betty, "eum adamavimus."

"Sed putet ad caelum," dixit mater eorum. "Vellem eum in calidarium lavandum confestim abduci."

Betty and Billy brought Walter home from the dog pound. "Nobody wanted him," said Billy.

"But we love him," said Betty.

"Well, he smells awful," said their mother. "I think you'd better give him a bath."

Eo perfecto mater ingressa, "Adhuc," inquit, "atrociter fetet."

Denique omnes intellegere coeperunt: bullae enim in aquo rem patefaciebant.

"Nimirum ille paulum veretur," dixit haec laetans, "atque venter eius dolet."

Walter autem ventre non est omnino affectus. Reapsa et ventre et cetero corpore plane valebat. Walter verum multum et saepe pedere solebat.

Mother walked in and said, "He still smells awful."

And that's when they got the first clue. The tell-tale bubbles in the water.

"He's probably just a little nervous," said Mother, hopefully. "His stomach must be upset."

But Walter's stomach wasn't upset. Walter's stomach was fine. He felt perfectly normal.

He just farted a lot.

Sic agebat cum lavaretur. Sic agebat ludens cum Betty et Billy. Sic agebat quandocumque domum perambularet;

cum in triclinio, tum in cucina item agebat. Etiam somnum capiens Walter pedere solebat.

He did it when he bathed. He did it when he played with Betty and Billy. He did it when he walked around the house. He did it in the dining room. He did it in the kitchen. And he did it in his sleep.

"Iste canis XXIV/VII/CCCLXV pedet," queritur pater.

"Non est potens sui, Tata," Betty Billyque aiunt, quibus nil interest si Walter pedat.

"Parvi refert si interdum ventum emittat," Billy dixit cum soli in suo conclavi cum Waltero congressi essent.

Betty quoque dixit caninos crepitus nullum negotium sibi praebere. Walter eiusdem scilicet animi innocens circumspiciebat, dum spatium suo odore subinde implebat.

"Fac eat ad medicum animalium," pater iussit.

"That dog farts morning, noon, and night," said Father.
    "He can't help it, Daddy," said Betty and Billy.
    They didn't mind Walter's farts.
    "So what if he farts," Billy said to Betty when they were alone in their room with Walter.
    Betty agreed. Walter agreed too. He sat there, looking innocently around, farting.

"Take him to the vet," said Father.

"Ventus," medicus affirmat. "Alias dictum, Intestina Tumida—ut nos in arte medicinae hunc morbum appellamus." Et eos admonuit ut victum ei commutarent.

"Farting," said the vet, "or rectal flatulence, as we say in the medical profession," and prescribed a change in diet.

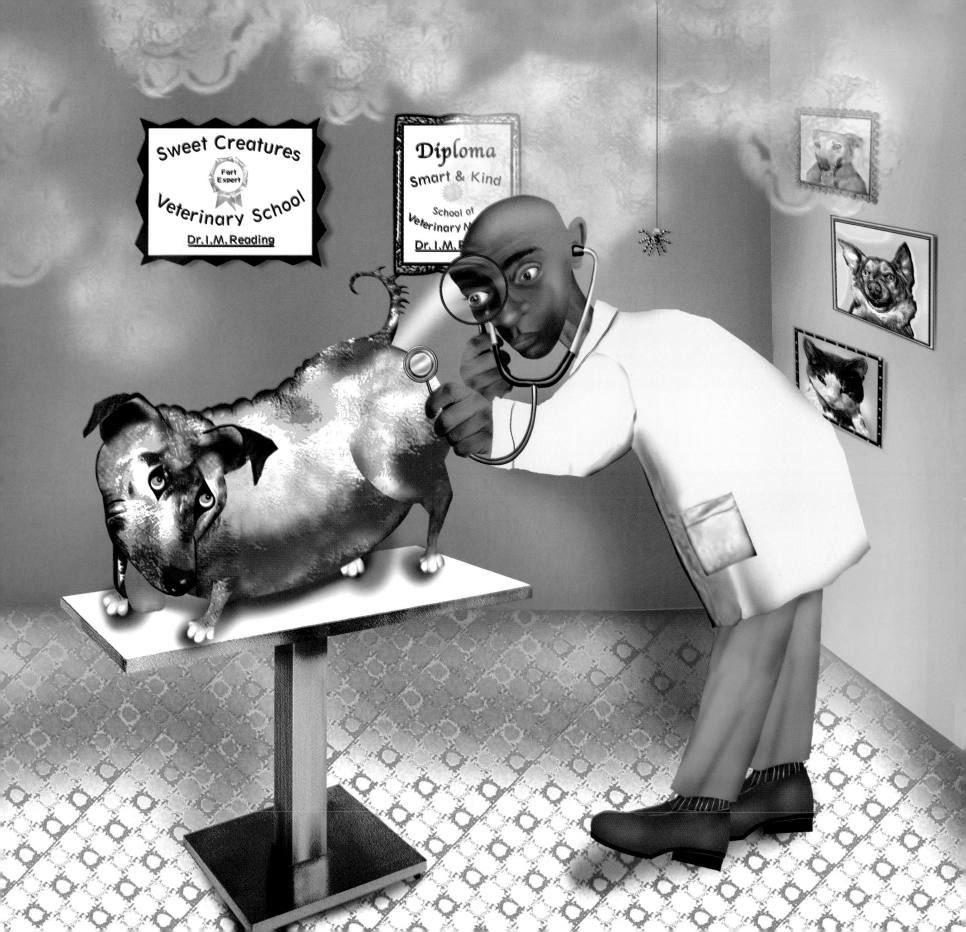

Proinde omni genere cibi canini Walterum pascunt—
nequiquam. Dehinc alimento felibus apto eum temptant. Tum
hillas ei insiciasque apponunt, et moreta lactucis
holeribusque commixta. Postea pullos coctos ei suppeditant.
Denique Walter offis cunicularibus pastus phytophagus fit.

"Quidquid iste canis edit, in odorem strepitusque obscenos commutat," pater summa voce declamat.

They gave Walter every kind of dog food. He farted. They tried him on cat food. They gave him hot dogs, hamburgers, and lettuce and tomato sandwiches. They gave him fried chicken. They gave him rabbit food. They made him a vegetarian.

"No matter what that dog eats, he turns it into farts," roared Father.

Etenim Walter ob crepitus alienos exinde culpari coepit. Nam si Avunculus Irv suppederet, tantum opus erat ut proxime eum adstaret et "Walter" proclamaret—et quisque suos oculos in hunc miserum simul vertebant.

Walter got the blame for everybody else's farts too. If Uncle Irv let one slip, he just went and stood near Walter.

Then all he had to say was, "Walter!"

And everyone would look at poor Walter.

"Nihil restat quin redeat unde eum inveneritis," dixit pater.
Betty autem, "Quaesimus," inquit, "ne eum dimittas."
Paterfamilias tamen "Cras ibit," affirmat.
Illi petebant, Walter pedebat.

Peractum est. Totam noctem Betty Billyque lacrimabant, dum Walter tristis vigilabat.
Tum Betty "O Walter," ait, "tibi non diutius pedendum est. Quia pater habet in animo te reduci ad canes domo egentes."

"He has to go back to the pound," said Father.
"No, Daddy, please," begged Betty and Billy. "Don't send Walter away."
"He goes tomorrow," said Father.
They pleaded. Walter farted.

It was all over. That night, Betty and Billy cried in their beds, and Walter looked at them unhappily.
"Oh Walter," said Betty, "you've got to stop farting."
"Because Father is going to send you back to the pound tomorrow," said Billy.

Walter cognovit quanti momenti res esset: numquam se iterum Betty Billyque visurum esse. Itaque constituit dehinc constanter crepitus cohibere. Donec Betty et Billy dormirent, ad cucinam descendit si quid edendum inveniret. Suo tenui eius naso effecit ut aperiret caliclarium reperiretque XXV librorum saccum paniciis caninis plenum quae tametsi a medico praescripta plus potius quam minus venti producerent. Et quamquam sciret quid eveniret, nequivit sibi temperare. Saccum vacuefecit et "Sapidissima" sibi dixit.

Walter knew how serious the situation was. He'd never see Betty and Billy again. He resolved to hold in his farts forever. When Betty and Billy fell asleep, he walked down to the kitchen to see if there was anything around to eat. He managed to open the cupboard door with his nose and found the 25-pound bag of low-fart dog biscuits the vet had prescribed for him, which had made him fart more. Even though he knew they made him fart more, he couldn't resist. He ate the entire bag. "Very tasty," said Walter to himself.

Ad lectum iaciturus se removit. Tum vastus ventus ventralis in eo crescere coepit. "Eheu," anxius censet, "hoc molestum videtur." Verebatur enim ne quid atrox eveniret ea emissa; nesciebat an domus ipsa disploderetur. Itaque eam in extremis maximoque cum labore continuit; nam ei constabat ne semel quidem rursus crepare. Reliquuum in tempus omnia ex hoc consistebant. Ibi iacebat, cauda inter femora compressa, cum clamorem ad fenestram audivit,

And then he went and lay down on the sofa. A gigantic gas bubble began to build inside him. "This is going to be trouble," he said to himself, nervously. He was afraid of what might happen if he let it go. He thought maybe the house would explode. So he kept it in. It wasn't easy. In fact, it was torture. But he had resolved never to fart again. His future depended on it. As he lay there, with his tail wrapped tightly between his legs, he heard a noise at the window.

tum eam lente aperiri vidit.

Duo fures sine sono in cucinam lapsi sunt.

Dein hic "Cave canem," dixit, sed ille "Non mordebit," respondit, "namque mollis mihi videtur." Walter quidem forsitan momordisset nisi tam inflatus esset ut vix moveri polleret. Ni latraret autem os panno vinxerunt.

"Nunc age" alter ait, "locum exhauriamus."

Unumquidque proximum rapuerunt. Walter impedivisset nisi quod ventre tam aegrotabat ut humi volveretur pedibus sublatis dentibusque stridentibus.

"Omnia iam adepti," alter dixit, "abeamus."

He watched it slowly open.

A pair of burglars came through.

They dropped silently into the kitchen.

"Watch out for the dog," said one of the burglars.

"He won't bite," said the other. "He's a wimp."

Walter might have bitten them, except he was so filled with gas he couldn't move. They tied a rag around his snout so he couldn't bark.

"Okay," whispered the first burglar, "let's clear the place out."

They took everything they could get their hands on. Walter wanted to stop them but he was having unbearable gas pains. He rolled on his back, and waved his paws in the air. He gnashed his teeth.

"We've got it all," said the second burglar.

"Let's go."

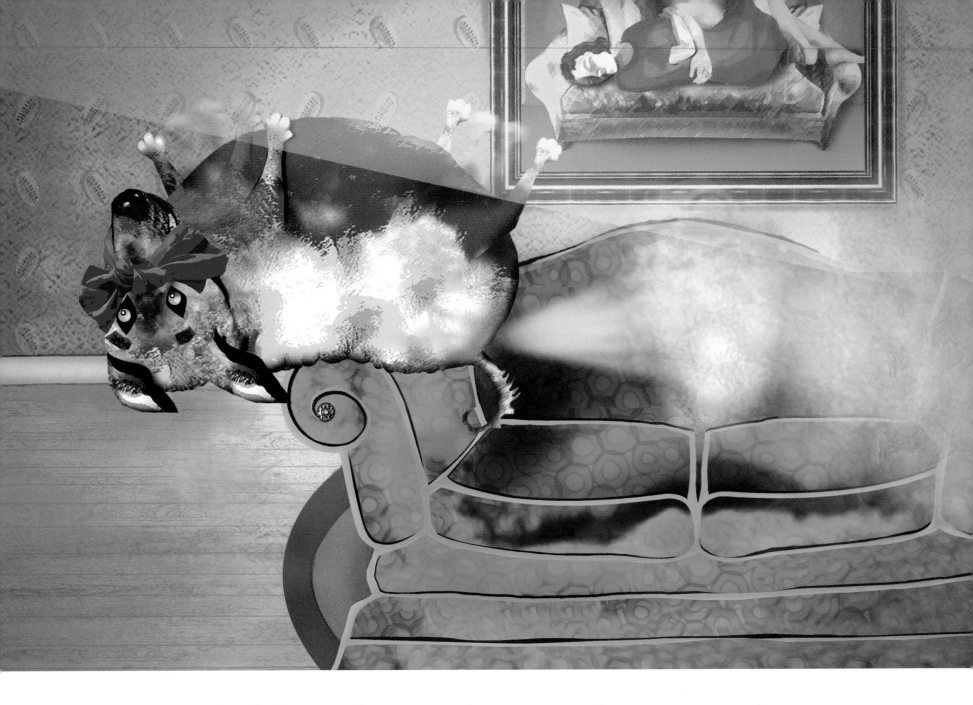

Deinde ibidem Walter pessimum aetatis suae strepitum emisit. Vasto cum stridore per conclavem sese propulsit foedissimo vento iam fartum. Fures suos ipsorum fauces deprehenderunt vix saltem spirantes. Oculis lacrimis suffusis ad fenestram festinaverunt. Cum saccum

aestimandis repletum secum vehere conati sint, vires et lacerti eos deficiebant. "Iam … iam … itur … ab … hinc … "

That's when Walter let it fly. It was the worst fart of his life. It made a tremendous noise and shot him across the room. A hideous cloud filled the air. The burglars clutched their throats, unable to breathe.

With tears in their eyes, they raced for the window. They tried to grab their bag with all the valuables in it, but their arms were too weak. "Let's … get … out … of … here … "

Ex fenestra salientes per vias decurrebant aegerrime suspirantes. Exinde noxio emissione adhuc caecati obvii lucernis currus vigilium occurrerunt.

"Fugam sistite statim," vigil imperavit.

They jumped out the window and ran up the block, choking and gasping for air. Still blinded by Walter's attack, they stepped into the headlights of an approaching police car.

"Hold it right there!" said the policeman.

Cum pater materque proximo die mane descenderant, fenestram apertam reppererunt. Saccum quoque suis aestimandis plenum creverunt. Walter quidem iuxta sedebat etiamnunc os panno devinctus. Dixeris eum fortissimum videri.

"Vasa argentea servavit!" mater clamavit.

Et "Quoque MQIOIPCVCI* servavit," addidit pater.

"Euge, Walter, optimus ac totus noster canis es, tametsi continuo pedas."

*Machina quae imagines omne in posterum captas visendi causa illustrat

When Father and Mother came down in the morning, they found the open window. And they saw the bag with their valuables in it. And Walter was sitting beside it. He still had the rag tied around his snout. You'd have to say he looked heroic.

"He saved the silverware!" cried Mother.

"He saved the VCR!" cried Father. "Good dog, Walter! You're our dog, even if you do fart all the time."

Itaque domum secum habitando assuefecit Walter—
Canis Gloriosus.
En coda fabulae nostrae.

And so the family learned to live with Walter, the hero dog.
And that's the end of our tail.